W9-CZA-247

Dear Parents:

Congratulations! Your child is taking the first steps on an exciting journey. The destination? Independent reading!

STEP INTO READING® will help your child get there. The program offers five steps to reading success. Each step includes fun stories and colorful art or photographs. In addition to original fiction and books with favorite characters, there are Step into Reading Non-Fiction Readers, Phonics Readers and Boxed Sets, Sticker Readers, and Comic Readers—a complete literacy program with something to interest every child.

Learning to Read, Step by Step!

Ready to Read   Preschool–Kindergarten
• big type and easy words • rhyme and rhythm • picture clues
For children who know the alphabet and are eager to begin reading.

Reading with Help   Preschool–Grade 1
• basic vocabulary • short sentences • simple stories
For children who recognize familiar words and sound out new words with help.

Reading on Your Own   Grades 1–3
• engaging characters • easy-to-follow plots • popular topics
For children who are ready to read on their own.

Reading Paragraphs   Grades 2–3
• challenging vocabulary • short paragraphs • exciting stories
For newly independent readers who read simple sentences with confidence.

Ready for Chapters   Grades 2–4
• chapters • longer paragraphs • full-color art
For children who want to take the plunge into chapter books but still like colorful pictures.

STEP INTO READING® is designed to give every child a successful reading experience. The grade levels are only guides; children will progress through the steps at their own speed, developing confidence in their reading. The F&P Text Level on the back cover serves as another tool to help you choose the right book for your child.

Remember, a lifetime love of reading starts with a single step!

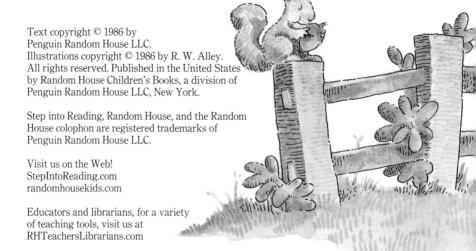

Visit us on the Web!
StepIntoReading.com
randomhousekids.com

Educators and librarians, for a variety
of teaching tools, visit us at
RHTeachersLibrarians.com

Library of Congress Cataloging-in-Publication Data
O'Connor, Jane.
The teeny tiny woman / retold by Jane O'Connor ; illustrated by R. W. Alley.
    p.   cm. — (Step into reading. A step 2 book)
Summary: A teeny tiny woman, who puts a teeny tiny bone she finds in a churchyard away in
a cupboard before she goes to sleep, is awakened by a voice demanding the return of the bone.
ISBN 978-0-394-88320-5 (trade) — ISBN 978-0-394-98320-2 (lib. bdg.)
[1. Ghosts—Folklore. 2. Folklore—England.]
I. Alley, R. W. (Robert W.), ill. II. Title. III. Step into reading. Step 2 book.
PZ8.1.O24 Te 2003 [E]—dc21   2002013448

Printed in the United States of America   65 64 63 62 61 60 59 58 57 56

This book has been officially leveled by using the F&P Text Level Gradient™ Leveling System.

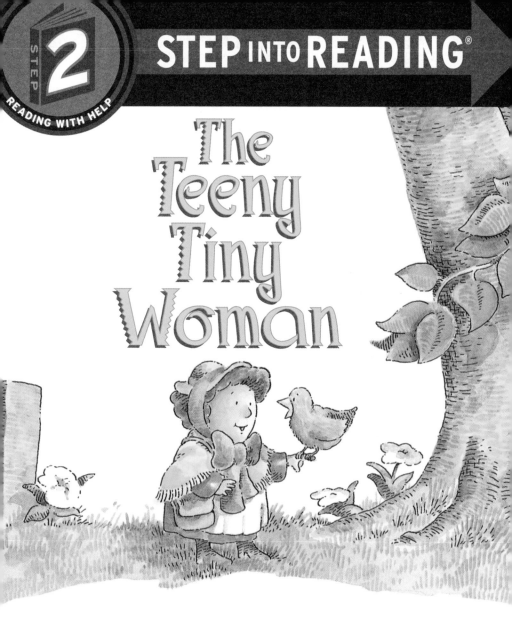

The Teeny Tiny Woman

retold by Jane O'Connor

illustrated by R. W. Alley

Random House 🏠 New York

A teeny tiny woman
lived in a teeny tiny house.

One day she put on
her teeny tiny hat.

She got her teeny tiny bag.

And she went for
a teeny tiny walk.

Soon the teeny tiny woman
came to a teeny tiny gate.

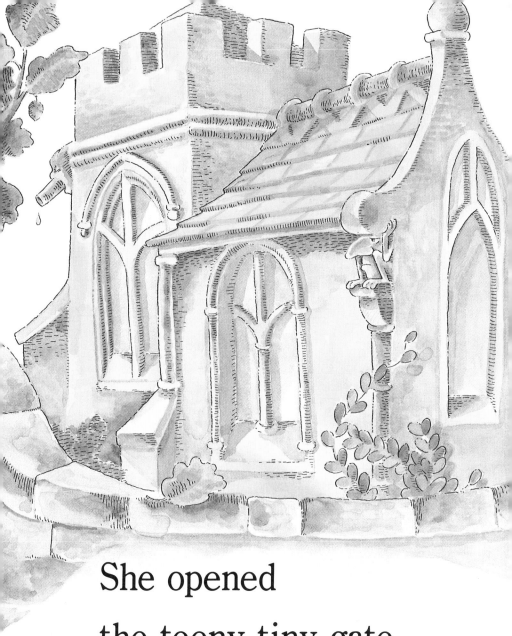

She opened
the teeny tiny gate
and went into
a teeny tiny yard.

There she saw
a teeny tiny bone
on a teeny tiny grave.
"I can make some
teeny tiny soup
with this teeny tiny bone,"
said the teeny tiny woman.

The teeny tiny woman
put the teeny tiny bone
in her teeny tiny bag.

She went through
the teeny tiny gate.

She walked
and walked
and walked
all the way back
to her teeny tiny house.

The teeny tiny woman
opened her teeny tiny door.

"My teeny tiny feet are tired,"
said the teeny tiny woman.

"I will not make
my teeny tiny soup now."

The teeny tiny woman
put the teeny tiny bone
in a teeny tiny cupboard.

Then she got into
her teeny tiny bed
for a teeny tiny nap.

Soon a teeny tiny
voice called:

"Give me my bone!"

The teeny tiny woman
was a teeny tiny bit scared.

"I must have had
a teeny tiny dream,"
she said.

The teeny tiny woman
had a teeny tiny glass
of milk.

Then she got back into
her teeny tiny bed.

Soon she fell asleep.

It was not long before
the teeny tiny voice
called out again.
"Give me my bone!"

The teeny tiny woman
woke up.

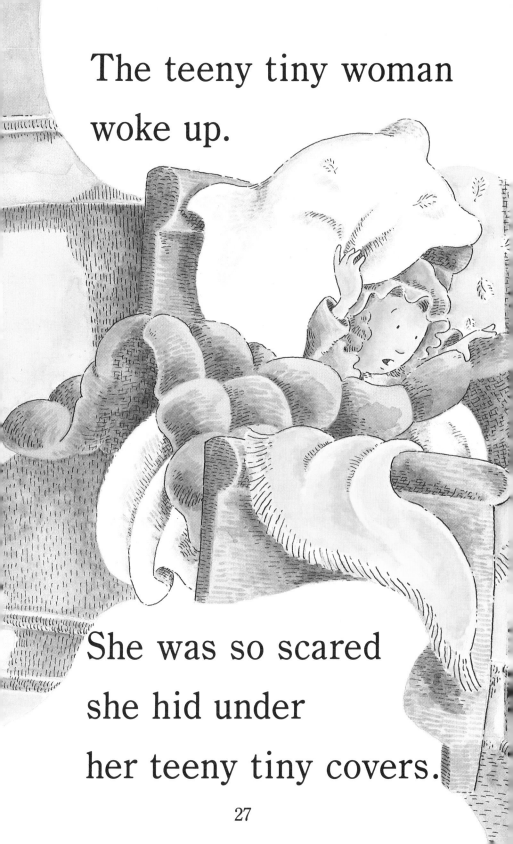

She was so scared
she hid under
her teeny tiny covers.

But the teeny tiny voice
called out again.
And now it was not
teeny tiny at all!

The teeny tiny woman
peeked out from
her teeny tiny covers.

And that is the end of
this teeny tiny story.